A CARTOON NETWORK ORIGINAL

ADVENTURE TIME

Finn and Jake's
ISLAND TRAVELOGUE

by Brandon T. Snider

CARTOON NETWORK
BOOKS

An Imprint of Penguin Random House

FINN & JAKE: WHO WE ARE & WHAT WE DO

What's up, Traveloguers?!
I'm Finn and I'll be your captain on this bjork'd-out voyage to exotic worlds beyond your comprehension. I'm pretty much an expert at trips, treks, and expeditions. Quests? I've gone on a few. When you've maneuvered through time and space as much as I have, you learn a thing or two. I've probably learned ten to twelve things **at least**. People can get pretty jelly of my incredible travel skillz, but I don't mind. I play to win. I've fought the Lich, kissed sweet princesses, and saved soooooo many lives. I'm, like, the biggest wig in the Land of Ooo. I also own a bunch of swords, and I've got super-luxurious hair. Had to get all of that out so you know I'm not a total shademeister who'll get you lost. I know what I'm doing. Now I present to you, dear reader, my faithful travel buddy . . .

I'm Jake. I'm pretty solid at voyaging and whatnot. I like ice cream, too.

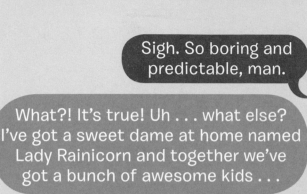

Sigh. So boring and predictable, man.

What?! It's true! Uh . . . what else? I've got a sweet dame at home named Lady Rainicorn and together we've got a bunch of awesome kids . . .

You're putting me to sleep, dude. Tell the people **what you can do**! Why are you the **ultimate travel companion**?!

I'd rather show 'em.

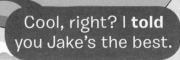

Cool, right? I **told** you Jake's the best.

THE MISSION: EXPLORING THE UNKNOWN

As reality-bending swashbucklers, Jake and I see it as our duty to share with you the secrets of **travel.** Today we're going on an excursion to a remote location filled with mystery, weirdness, and crazy critters that'll make you question everything you know about **everything.**

Where are we going? Tell me! Tell me!

Hold your horses, Jake. First we've got to establish the deets on this whole mission, and that's **exploration.** We're here to see new places and try new stuff. It's pretty much what life is all about. That and piping-hot burritos. We'll be investigating a place that's rarely been seen by outside eyes. Aw, man, you are sooooo lucky. You ready to study some nooks and crannies? Whatever happens, don't be afraid. Jake and I have totally got your back. Do you know what we're searching for, Jake?

The truth?

Yeah, but there's more to it than that.

Myself?

Totally, but not right **now**.

The lost diaries of Captain Taco?

Okay, now you're losing focus. We're searching for **the Unknown**.

What's the Unknown?

We just don't know.

THE ISLANDS: WHAT? WHERE? HUH?

Now that I've revealed that our venture is into **the Unknown,** you're probably asking yourself, "Seriously, where are we going?!?! I don't want to leave my tree house! I don't want to put on pants! I want to stay at home and feed my face like a blubbery goo monster!!" First of all—it's a good thing you're going on a trip because **you need to seriously chill.** Second of all—we're heading to a bunch of mysterious **islands!**

I love mysteries. And islands. Both of them together? Mind-blowing.

Our ultimate destination is **Founders' Island.** She's beautiful, right? Jake and I are going to tell you **all** about how to get there. We'll have to go to a bunch of other places first. I hope you're okay with that. Like I said, **relax.** We've got everything covered.

Wait a second. If we know where we're going, then how is it **the Unknown**? That doesn't make sense. We know, man. **We know.**

Stop being difficult and go with the flow here.

Sigh. Okay.

PREPPIN' FOR THE TREK

> Preppin' for the trek, preppin' for the trek . . .

Before you head out into **the Unknown,** you're going to want to make sure you have everything you need. Stop worrying, ya worrywart! Jake and I are going to take you through all the junk 'n' bunk you'll need for your wild adventure across the vastness of the open sea. It's going to take guts. I hope you're filled with tons of guts because Founders' Island isn't some dumb ol' resort with a pool and fruity drinks; it's **so much more.** Things could get . . . dicey. Pay attention and let the **master wayfarers** speak.

> Is that **us**? I like it.

We're going to cover a lot of ground, so **listen up.** First, you're going to need a **squad** made up of your closest and most amazing friends. Make sure you trust whoever you bring with you. That way they won't bolt when things get a little bloobalooby.

Then you're going to need **transportation.** How else are you going to get where you're going, silly? Choosing the right way to travel isn't easy, especially when you don't have a lot of options. But whatever happens, **don't** hitch a ride with a chatty ocean worm. It might not end well for you. More on that later.

Yeah, yeah, yeah, but what do I need to **bring**?

I'm glad you asked, Jake. **Gear** is essential to exploring. You can't bring a lot of it, so think about the stuff you **need.** Bring stuff that will help you when you're in a bind.

Nail clippers. Nail clippers for sure.

I've got something to say about this whole thing. When is it my turn to talk?

Uhhhhhhh, now I guess? Make it quick.

Who's going to look after the Tree Fort while we're gone?

Very good question, Jake. Which brings me to a point that I forgot to make but am going to make right now. Before you leave for any expedition, make sure someone is around to watch your stuff! Especially if your stuff is cool. You definitely don't want it to get stolen.

Hey, you know who was really good at watching over the Land of Ooo when we were on our trip last time? **Fern.** He's dependable, heroic, and responsible; he doesn't steal stuff; he's a positive thinker; and he's also got a killer smile. Best of all? He's **available.** Do **you**, Fern!

Jake, my friend, what a solid idea. You're a brilliant explorer who's def worth his salt.

How much is salt worth?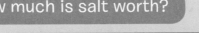

It's an expression, man.

I know that, but I'm asking a real question.

Uhhhh. I don't know. Probably, like, two cents.

I've got two cents!

Jake's Two Cents

Make sure you give your girl a big wet smooch before you leave for your trip!

 Now turn the page to **assemble the squad!**

SQUAD FILES

NAME: BMO

NICKNAME: Beemo, B. Diddy, The Mod

There are a million and one reasons to bring BMO along on your travels. I can't go over all of them, so I'll cover the most important ones. Do you like to laugh? BMO will make you crack up like you heard the longest, loudest, most hilarious toot of all time. Do you like to dance to music? BMO **can go all night.** Most importantly, do you like trusting your life to a giggly little game console who is all about making you smile even when you feel like punching a pile of dirt because you're mad about a girl? BMO will watch over you to make sure you don't fall into a pit of craziness. It's really that simple. And if you choose not to follow my directions, it doesn't even matter because BMO will hide in your boat, anyway, and surprise you when you least expect it.

BMO! BMO! BMO! BMO!

Let's go to your happy place! **I'll drive.**

SQUAD FILES

NAME: ~~Susan Strong~~ Kara

SOMETIMES KNOWN AS: XJ-7-7

If you're doing some globetrotting (and I know you are because that's why you're here), I can't think of anyone better to bring along than our favorite gal, **Susan Strong**. Hey, that kind of rhymes. Anyway, she's the best. Susan's got a heart of gold and the spirit of a true warrior. When push comes to shove, she'll shove that push like nobody's business. She doesn't take blorps from anyone, if you know what I mean (and I think you do). Susan kicks major tushy, and that's all there is to say about that. **And** she gets bonus points for reconnecting with her past. Susan doesn't just know about island travel; she **lives, breathes,** and **eats** it.

Susan! Susan! Susan! Susan!

Always bring a fresh bathing suit. **Or else.**

TRANSPORTATION

How do you get to your island destination? I'm glad you asked. Shall we review some options . . . ?

We shall.

Air

Some people prefer to travel in a mysterious flying stingray-mobile that shows up out of nowhere and shoots crazy little mini stingray thingies onto people's faces and grabs strangers with its creepy tentacles. But that's **some** people. Do what works for **you.**

Sea

How about getting yourself a sturdy seafaring vessel for your voyage? P Bubbs lent us her sweet ride, *Sugar Spit*, because she's an awesome person who can build a candy boat with her eyes closed and her hands tied behind her back. But then stuff happened, *Sugar Spit* went kaput, and Jake became our ship. It happens.

HOW TO TAME THE SALTY SEA OF SURE DEATH WITH FINN & JAKE

Getting to **any** island involves riding the waves. That's part of the gig, dude. Trust me, I'm a **sea dawg.** I know these things. I was afraid of the sea for a long time, but my fears were swept away when the **winds of change** blew through.

 Whoa, man. That's deep.

Not as deep as the ocean. That's why you've got to be careful. Treat the sea with respect. Sing it an old song to calm it down.

"Hush little ocean, don't get all wavy! Jake is gonna buy you a guy named Davey!"

 Uhhhhhh, sure.

Get yourself a pocket sextant! It's a sweet little doodad that'll help you navigate the open ocean. I keep mine in my belly folds for easy access. **Don't judge.**

CREATURES OF THE DEEP

You're going to see **a lot** of dippy sea critters in your travels. **Don't freak out.** Some of them are totally harmless. Like Jake!

Hey, I'm not harmless. I can harm if I want to.

I know, man. I'm just joshing you.

And I'm not a dippy sea critter, either.

I was joshing about that, too!

Yeah, whatever. I don't like all this joshing.

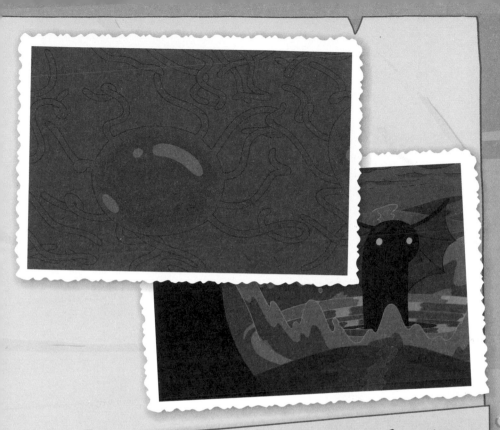

Jake's Two Cents

Watch out for jellyfish!!! They'll attach themselves to your tummy and use their gross jellyfish poison to jack up your perception of reality. I thought I saw my parents! But it was really some dumb old seaweed. Why do jellyfish do that?! It's pretty rude, if you ask me.

MEET WHIPPLE THE HAPPY DRAGON (AND THEN LEAVE)

One thing to keep in mind when you're on a journey: **Always expect the unexpected.** If you saw a giant slithering sea worm in the distance, you'd probably be afraid, right? What if I told you that was some happy dragon who'll try to pitch you a screenplay idea about a hot turtle couple who are actually gophers?

I'd call that **unexpected**.

Exactly. So keep an eye out for **Whipple the Happy Dragon.** He's the only dragon you'll come across that's actually happy, even though I think he's also sorta lonely. (Must be tough being out there on your own. That's probably why he can't stop talking.) Don't make him mad, or he'll fire up that **wind bladder** of his and create a crazy water vortex that'll throw you off course. Smile and nod as much as possible. Tell him he's pretty. He'll **love** that.

GEAR

Make sure you pack a couple of pairs of earplugs. They're the perfect thing for when Whipple tells you his dreams over and over and over again.

Sea lizard make scary storm magic!

Find yourself . . .

with

CAP'N NAV!

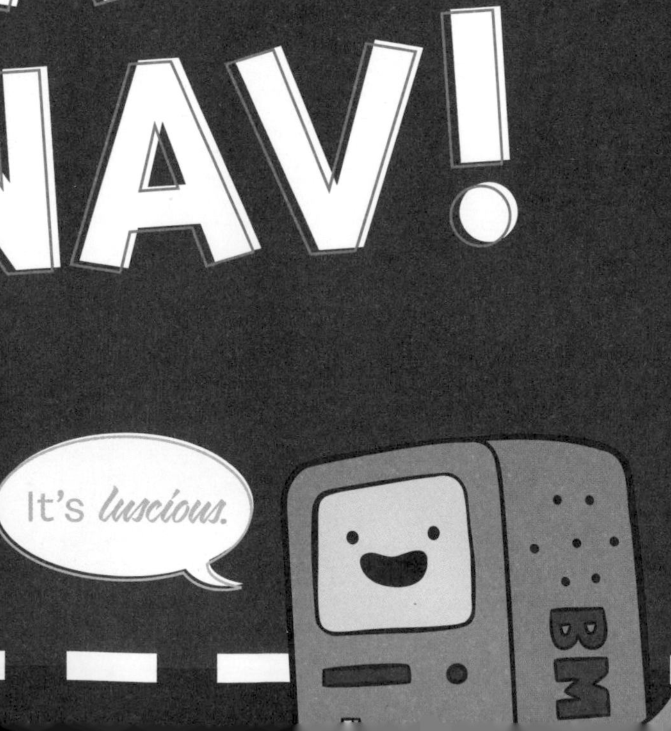

PAID ADVERTISEMENT FOR CAP'N NAV APP

STUFF YOU MIGHT ENCOUNTER DURING YOUR VOYAGE . . .

Pygmy Elephants & an Active Volcano

Those weirdos better watch out for **hot lava!**

Cat Rock

It's chubby cat-shaped!

Poison Reef

It's a reef that is **very** poison-y!

Peril, Danger & Jeopardy

Oh no! BMO hates **Peril, Danger & Jeopardy**! Take me back to my hotel room!

BEWARE THE COLOSSUS OF THE DEEP

WELCOME TO THE ISLANDS!

Dude, we made it!

I'm exhausted.

Once you arrive at your destination, take a breather! But only for a second. **Then** you should thoroughly observe your surroundings. You never know if there are creepers lurking around. It's always a good thing to get **the lay of the land**.

How do you do that?

It's simple. Take a look around. Open those sparkling peepers, and behold the glory of your isle retreat.

What if there are creepers lurking where I can't see?

Hmmmm. Good question. I suggest you whip out your charming wit and tell some jokes. That should bring 'em out of hiding.

What if they think my jokes are stinky?

Oh, well, if that happens, **run for your life**.

Hey, where's BMO?

KNOW YOUR FAUNA

What's *fauna*?

Fauna are all the animals that live in a specific region. And there are some **weird animals** in these here islands. **Prepare to battle them like the mighty warrior you are.** It might not come to all of that, but you never know. Be prepared.

When annoying **crabs** come at you with the *clickety clack*, be ready to shout 'em back! Oh, and ask them for me if they're robots, wouldja? I've got questions.

Riding a **giant bird** seems like a bad idea at first, but once you get up into the sky it becomes the exhilarating thrill ride of a lifetime. What I'm saying is . . . **do it.**

The most important thing you will ever hear in your entire life is this: **Giant bears** are gonna use your flute to scratch their butts and **then** they will smell that flute. **I know.** I couldn't believe it myself, but here we are. **And** they've got stank breath. Makes sense.

GEOGRAPHY: WHERE AM I?

Knowing the geography of the place you're visiting is pretty important. It'll help you navigate the area a whole lot easier. Trust me on this. I've climbed a lot of stuff in my time. Here's Jake to tell you more . . .

WEATHER: WHAT'S FALLING FROM THE SKY RIGHT NOW?

Make sure you check the weather forecast before you leave your Tree Fort. That way you'll know what kind of clothes to pack for your adventure. You don't want to show up to a sizzling hot beach wearing a snowsuit. You'll end up a sweaty cotton ball.

Weather is crazy, am I right? There's **rain**, which is like water falling from the sky and stuff. Gettin' everything wet like a bunch of moisture or something. Crazy **rain.**

Then there's **wind**, blowin' everything all around and whatnot, messin' up people's hair.

Snow is like **rain** but all cold and mushy. Brrrrrr. I'm chilly just thinkin' about it.

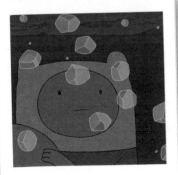

Hail is like **snow** except hard and mean. Dumb hail, always hittin' me in the head.

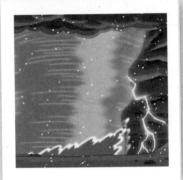

Watch out for twisters!!!

Dude, you act like you've never experienced weather before. Chill. Not in the **cold** way, but in the **cool** way.

GEAR

When it's too cold for you to go outside, grab yourself a burlap sack and some seed packets. Throw 'em together, and you've got yourself a nice outfit that can withstand freezing temperatures . . . but only for a couple of minutes. It's actually not that great of an idea but, hey, you work with what you got, right?

TRAPS: BEWARE OF THEM

Sometimes, when you're exploring **the Unknown**, minding your business, looking for someone, **anyone**, that can help you because you got separated from your travel buddies, you might **accidentally** fall into a trap. **Don't panic. Stay calm.** As a matter of fact, hang out for a while and enjoy your new surroundings. Get to know the other poor little creatures who got trapped alongside you. And if you happen to see that butt-flute-sniffing bear, make a desperate appeal for help. He'll probably say no and keep sniffing that butt-flute, but you should try, anyway. Someone'll be along soon. Keep hope alive.

Let's Meet Alva!

LIKES: Watching old movies, junk 'n' relics from the past, board games, flutes

DISLIKES: Strangers, powerful winds, strangers who try to pillage her home

FUN FACT: She will steal a dude's backpack and not think twice.

If you get separated from your squad, **don't panic.** Someone will help you eventually (if you scream loud enough). When I got lost, I ended up meeting this really cool lady named **Alva.** I say "meet," but I really mean that she caught me in a net like I was food. Alva is a local gal, doing her thing, tryin' to stay alive on a topsy-turvy island of adventure. Once she knew I wasn't a bad guy, she welcomed me with open arms, inviting me into her awesome, teched-out tree house. **Look at that thing.** I learned that even though someone traps you in a net, it doesn't mean they want to cook you up for dinner. It means they're being careful. Don't take it personally if Alva doesn't talk to you. She's the strong, silent type.

JAKE'S TIPS FOR BEING A GOOD GUEST

Whether you're visiting an old friend in your hometown or making a new buddy on a planet in another galaxy, **always** make sure you're being a super-solid guest. Look up local customs before you get to your destination. That way you'll be able to greet new people the way they're used to being greeted. People are different wherever you go, and it's important to accept those differences. Dude, go ahead and embrace them! Open up your heart and your mind to other cultures. I'm tellin' you, you won't regret it.

Deeeeeeeeeeeeep.

TIP #1

Don't be afraid to chow down on exotic delicacies! Heh . . .

TIP #2

Compliment your host on her fashion sense! Lookin' bundled, Alva. **Very cool.**

TIP #3

Could your accommodations use a fresh cleanup? Offer a helping hand to your host. Maybe they're too busy to clean, you know? People get busy.

HISTORY LESSON: HYOOMANS

It's important to do your research when traveling to new places, even if those places are a mystery. Learn about the people you'll be interacting with as much as possible. **Be respectful.** You're a stranger in a strange land, not the other way around.

Tell 'em about the Hyoomans, tell 'em about the Hyoomans.

I'm on it, Jake. The Hyooman Tribe is a group of odd-looking folks who Jake and I met when we stumbled upon their subterranean lair. That's how we met **Susan.** We had **a lot** of questions at first. You've probably got some yourself. The thing about the Hyoomans is that they're pretty much a mystery. Susan didn't know about her past and how she and the Hyoomans came to be. When we set out on our trek across the islands, we expected to meet a Hyooman or two but there was **a lot** more in store for us than we imagined. We'll get to **that** a little bit later. Be patient.

Where is Susan, anyway?

Sometimes, when you're on a journey, you accidentally get caught in a super-crazy storm and lose one of your squad. If that happens, **don't freak out.** I can't say that enough. Losing track of a squad member just means you'll have to go on a little detour to find 'em and bring 'em back. It's not always easy. BMO likes to get caught up in this wacky VR fantasyland where you can pretty much do anything you want. It's distracting, especially when you're on a mission. Jake and I hate to have to pull BMO out of it, but we've got to get back on track and stay the course. **No squad members left behind.**

BMO has a whole other life going on in there, man.

We're the ones who are going to shake our pal out of the ultimate fantasyland. It's an annoying job, but someone's got to do it. You ready to venture into crazy town, Jake?

Yeah! Unknown, here we come!

We've been there before, dude.

I know. I just needed to psych myself up.

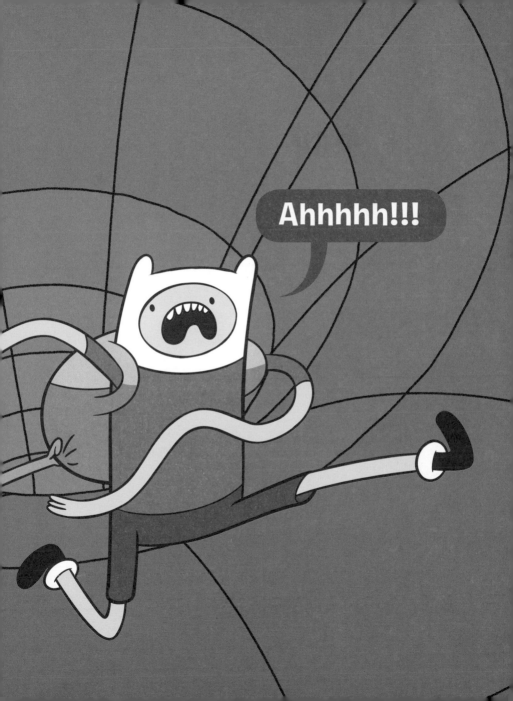

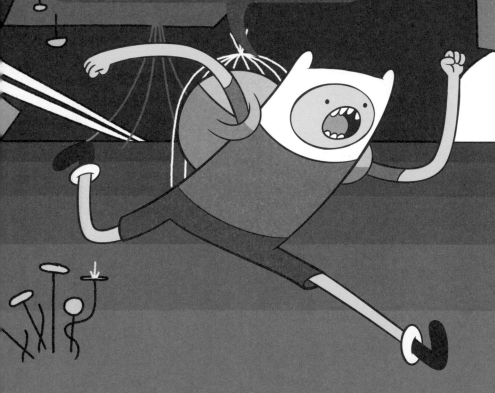

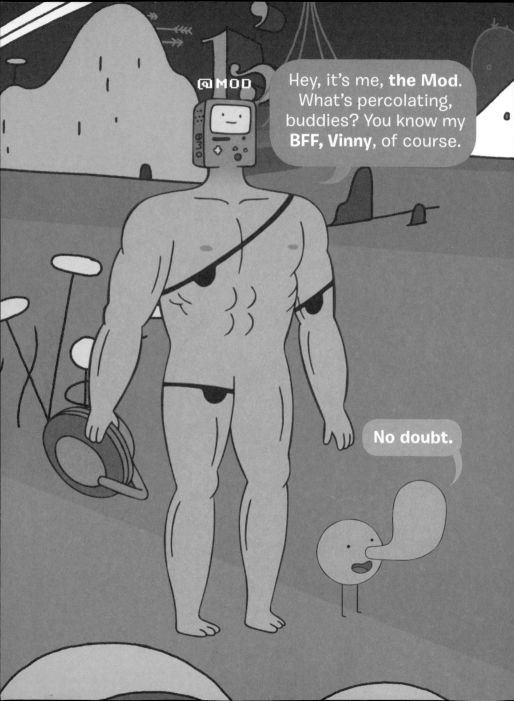

We're on a mission here, BMO, uh, I mean **the Mod**. There's no time for a VR detour right now. Say good-bye to your pals, and we'll drop you back here later. Promise.

Shucks. Oh well. When duty calls, BMO answers. (Hello, duty? Don't worry, I'm coming!) Peace out, Vinny.

Catch ya on the flip side, squirt.

Back to life, back to reality.

How much longer till we get to our destination? I'm hungry, and I think I might need to tinkle.

Don't be that guy, Jake.

FOUNDERS' ISLAND!

Hey! We're here! Whoa. I think I'm still a little woozy from that VR world.

Welcome to Founders' Island! This place is crawling with weird history. A **long** time ago, there were these people called **Hiders** and there were these other people called **Seekers**. There were also **Helpers**, but we're not there yet. Hey, wait a minute . . .

Susan's back!

Kara. I was once called **Kara.**

Uhhhhhhhh, yeah. Cool. So, um, back to the whole **Hiders and Seekers** thing. It's kind of complicated . . .

 Just play the Founders' song, man.

THE FOUNDERS' SONG

We had to leave our place because the world was dyin' and everyone that wasn't dead spent all of their time cryin'...

Our ways had failed, nature had failed, we made a lot of errors . . .

FOUNDERS' SONG (CONTINUED)

The Founders had some new ideas that
made everything better . . .

The Founders dreamed of this island; our ships landed on its shore. They built our wonderful guardian to keep destruction from our door.

Who came up with this song? It's weird.

Some lady named **Dr. Gross**. From what I hear, she's wacky.

The Hiders fear these new ideas, but do your best to help them. Cuz just outside is darkness and death, disease, monsters, and problems.

So come out of your hiding place, come out of the darkness, and we'll find a new way to live by the light of the Founders!

HUB ISLAND

Hub Island is where people trained to be Seekers. Then it was abandoned.

Stop. I can't watch anymore!

Is Kara okay?

No, Kara is **not** okay. Also, I want to be called **Susan.**

Uhhhh, okay. That's cool.

Everything I knew about my past was wrong! Founders' Island was once my home. I was happy here. But then I was given an implant that affected my mind and made me do things I didn't want to do. I was controlled and manipulated to believe something that wasn't the whole truth. I was denied my **freedom.**

Denying people freedom is the worst.

I was denied **choices.** I was unable to **explore** or **learn new things.** Everything was decided for me. **I had no free will.**

This is getting really intense, dude.

SUSAN & FRIDA: FRIENDS 4 LIFE

But **Frida** helped me see the light through the darkness. She's my best friend. Frida dreamed of freedom and knew that there was more to life than the islands. I didn't believe her. My mind was too cloudy with mumbo jumbo. She wanted to find her true self and see the world! Then *I* put a stop to it. But **now** we're both free to travel together and go **adventuring** on our own. **We're free to make new memories together!**

Sometimes, when you go on a quest, you reconnect with old friends. It's an awesome feeling. And sometimes, when you go on a quest, you reconnect with something **more**. Susan wasn't the only person to have her past revealed to her. Yep. That's right. **I've got a secret origin.**

THE SECRET ORIGIN OF FINN MERTENS

Starring
Minerva Campbell

This lady right here? This is **my mom.** Her name is Minerva. She's from Founders' Island. I didn't know her for a very long time. She's kind, sympathetic, and really good at science. Like . . . **really good.** My dad was an irresistible old flirt who charmed his way into her heart. He was a complicated man. A clumsy gadgeteer. Okay, he was a **con man.** But their love produced **me,** a buff little bionic baby! And then things changed. It's a **long story.**

Sorry to interrupt your moment, bro. But we need to wrap up this whole thing. We still have to tell the secret origin of the whole island thingiemawhoo before we head home.

I can help with that . . .

THE SECRET ORIGIN OF THE ISLAND

I'll take it from here, son. After Finn disappeared, all I did was work. It helped me cope with his loss. You remember Dr. Gross from before, yeah? Well, her irresponsible behavior led to the release of a terrible virus that was disastrous for our species. We did the best we could to contain the situation, but we suffered much loss. I was a Helper. That's what I did. So I uploaded my brain map to the web and into these Minerva Bots. I did it to save humanity and have been doing it ever since. Now that Finn has returned, I do believe my outlook has changed for the better. I'm starting to see life in a brand-new light. Well . . . you two better run along now. It seems we've all got work to do.

 She's right! We've got to get back home. **Bye, Mom!**

Awwwwwww, **dude.** The end of vacations are the **worst**.

That's the truth.

You still there, **Traveloguers**? I know we threw **a lot** of stuff your way. Thanks for handling it all so well. If you made it through this experience in one piece, ask yourself some important questions: Did I try new stuff? What did I learn? Did I meet new people? What did they teach me? Did I watch a bear scratch his butt with a flute and then smell the flute? How did it affect me as a person?

I learned that **freedom** is awesome. I also think I lost my nail clippers. Anyway, let's go home. All this stuff is making me miss my family. Man, I love them **so much**.

All right, Jake. It's time to get this show on the road.

BEWARE THE GUARDIAN

Gah! I forgot about **the Guardian of the Islands.**

Smell ya later, ya donk!

Don't make him mad, Jake.

Sorry. You know, we've been traveling for so long, I think I forget what Ooo looks like.

I haven't forgotten . . .

Ain't no party like a Land of Ooo party cuz a Land of Ooo party is **crazy.**